Bert Leston Taylor

A Line-o´-Verse or Two

I0599284

Outlook

Bert Leston Taylor

A Line-o´-Verse or Two

1. Auflage | ISBN: 978-3-73262-680-9

Erscheinungsort: Frankfurt am Main, Deutschland

Erscheinungsjahr: 2018

Outlook Verlag GmbH, Frankfurt.

A Line-o'-Verse or Two

By

Bert Leston Taylor

The Reilly & Britton Co.

Chicago

NOTE

For the privilege of reprinting the rimes gathered here I am indebted to the courtesy of the *Chicago Tribune* and *Puck*, in whose pages most of them first appeared. "The Lay of St. Ambrose" is new.

One reason for rounding up this fugitive verse and prisoning it between covers was this: Frequently—more or less—I receive a request for a copy of this jingle or that, and it is easier to mention a publishing house than to search through ancient and dusty files.

The other reason was that I wanted to.

B. L. T.

TO MY READERS

Not merely of this book,—but a larger company, with whom, through the medium of the Chicago Tribune, *I have been on very pleasant terms for several years,—this handful of rime is joyously dedicated.*

THE LAY OF ST. AMBROSE

"*And hard by doth dwell, in St. Catherine's cell,
Ambrose, the anchorite old and grey.*"

Ambrose the anchorite old and grey
    Larruped himself in his lonely cell,
And many a welt on his pious pelt
    The scourge evoked as it rose and fell.

For hours together the flagellant leather
    Went whacketty-whack with his groans of pain;
And the lay-brothers said, with a wag of the head,
"Ambrose has been at the bottle again."

And such, in sooth, was the sober truth;
    For the single fault of this saintly soul
Was a desert thirst for the cup accurst,—
    A quenchless love for the Flowing Bowl.

When he woke at morn with a head forlorn
    And a taste like a last-year swallow's nest,
He would kneel and pray, then rise and flay
    His sinful body like all possessed.

Frequently tempted, he fell from grace,
    And as often he found the devil to pay;
But by diligent scourging and diligent purging
    He managed to keep Old Nick at bay.

This was the plight of our anchorite,—
    An endless penance condemned to dree,—
When it chanced one day there came his way
    A Mystical Book with a golden Key.

This Mystical Book was a guide to health,
    That none might follow and go astray;
While a turn of the Key unlocked the wealth
    That all unknown in the Scriptures lay.

Disease is sin, the Book defined;
    Sickness is error to which men cling;
Pain is merely a state of mind,
    And matter a non-existent thing.

If a tooth should ache, or a leg should break,
    You simply "affirm" and it's sound again.
Cut and contusion are only delusion,
    And indigestion a fancied pain.

For pain is naught if you "hold a thought,"
  Fevers fly at your simple say;
You have but to affirm, and every germ
  Will fold up its tent and steal away.

━━━━━━

From matin gong to even-song
  Ambrose pondered this mystic lore,
Till what had seemed fiction took on a conviction
  That words had never possessed before.

"If pain," quoth he, "is a state of mind,
  If a rough hair shirt to silk is kin,—
If these things are error, pray where's the terror
  In scourging and purging oneself of sin?

"It certainly seemeth good to me,
  By and large, in part and in whole.
I'll put it in practice and find if it fact is,
  Or only a mystical rigmarole."

━━━━━━

The very next night our anchorite
  Of the Flowing Bowl drank long and deep.
He argued this wise: "New Thought applies
  No fitter to lamb than it does to sheep."

When he woke at morn with a head forlorn
  And a taste akin to a parrot's cage,
He knelt and prayed, then up and flayed
  His sinful flesh in a righteous rage.

Whacketty-whack on breast and back,
  Whacketty-whack, before, behind;
But he held the thought as he laid it on,
  "Pain is merely a state of mind."

Whacketty-whack on breast and back,
  Whacketty-whack on calf and shin;
And the lay-brothers said, with a wag of the head,
  "*Ain't* he the glutton for discipline!"

4

Now every night our anchorite
  Was exceedingly tight when he went to bed.
The scourge that once pained him no longer restrained him,
  Nor even the fear of an aching head.

For he woke at morn with a pate as clear
  As the silvery chime of the matinbell;
And without any jogging he fell to his flogging,
  And larruped himself in his lonely cell.

But the leather had lost its power to sting;
  To pangs of the flesh he was now immune;
His rough hair shirt no longer hurt,
  Nor the pebbles he wore in his wooden shoon.

When conscience was troubled he cheerfully doubled
  His matinal dose of discipline;—
A deuce of a scourging, sufficient for purging
  The Devil himself of original sin.

Whacketty-whack on breast and back,
  Whacketty-whack from morn to noon;
Whacketty-whacketty-whacketty-whack!—
  Till the abbey rang with the dismal tune.

Deacon and prior, lay-brother and friar
  Exclaimed at these whoppingsspectacular;
And even the Abbot remarked that the habit
  Of scourging oneself might be carried too far.

"My son," said he, "I am pleased to see
  Such penance as never was known before;
But you raise such a racket in dusting your jacket,
  The noise is becoming a bit of a bore.

"How would it do if you whaled yourself
  From eight to ten or from one to three?
Or if 'More' is your motto, pray hire a grotto;
  I know of one you can have rent free."

Ambrose the anchorite bowed his head,

And girded his loins and went away.
He rented a cavern not far from a tavern,
And tippled by night and scourged by day.

The more the penance the more the sin,
The more he whopped him the more he drank;
Till his hair fell out and his cheeks fell in,
And his corpulent figure grew long and lank.

At Whitsuntide he up and died,
While flaying himself for his final spree.
And who shall say whether 'twas liquor or leather
That hurried him into eternity?

They made him a saint, as well they might,
And gave him a beautiful aureole.
And—somehow or other, this circle of light
Suggests the rim of the Flowing Bowl.

TO A TALL SPRUCE

Pride of the forest primeval,
Peer of the glorious pine,
Doomed to an end that is evil,
Fearful the fate that is thine!

Peer of the glorious pine,
Now the landlooker has found you,
Fearful the fate that is thine—
Fate of the spruces around you.

Now the landlooker has found you,
Stripped of your beautiful plume—
Fate of the spruces around you—
Swiftly you'll draw to your doom.

Stripped of your beautiful plume,
Bzzng! into logs they will whip you.
Swiftly you'll draw to your doom;
To the pulp mill they will ship you.

Bzzng! into logs they will whip you,
Lumbermen greedy for gold.
To the pulp mill they will ship you.

Hearken, there's worse to be told!

Lumbermen greedy for gold
Over your ruins will caper.
Hearken, there's worse to be told:
You will be made into paper!

Over your ruins will caper
Murderous shavers and hooks.
You will be made into paper!
You will be made into books!

Murderous shavers and hooks
Swiftly your pride will diminish.
You will be made into books!
Horrible, horrible finish!

Swiftly your pride will diminish.
You will become a romance!
Horrible, horrible finish!
Fate has no sadder mischance.

You will become a romance,
Filled with "Gadzooks!" and "Have at you!"
Fate has no sadder mischance;
It would wring tears from a statue.

Filled with "Gadzooks!" and "Have at you!"
You may become a "Lazarre"—
(It would wring tears from a statue)—
"Graustark," "Stovepipe of Navarre."

You may become a "Lazarre";
Fate has still worse it can turn on—
"Graustark," "Stovepipe of Navarre,"
Even a "Dorothy Vernon"!

Fate has still worse it can turn on—
Lower you cannot descend;
Even a "Dorothy Vernon"!—
That is the limit—the end.

Lower you cannot descend.
Doomed to an end that is evil,
That *is* the limit—the *end*!
Pride of the forest primeval.

IN THE LAMPLIGHT

The dinner done, the lamp is lit,
And in its mellow glow we sit
And talk of matters, grave and gay,
That went to make another day.
Comes Little One, a book in hand,
With this request, nay, this command—
(For who'd gainsay the little sprite)—
"Please—will you read to me to-night?"

Read to you, Little One? Why, yes.
What shall it be to-night? You guess
You'd like to hear about the Bears—
Their bowls of porridge, beds and chairs?
Well, that you shall.... There! that tale's done!
And now—you'd like another one?
To-morrow evening, Curly Head.
It's "hass-pass seven." Off to bed!

So each night another story: Wicked
dwarfs and giants gory; Dragons
fierce and princes daring, Forth to
fame and fortune faring; Wandering
tots, with leaves for bed; Houses
made of gingerbread; Witches bad
and fairies good,
And all the wonders of the wood.

"I like the witches best," says she
Who nightly nestles on my knee;
And why by them she sets such store,
Psychologists may puzzle o'er.
Her likes are mine, and I agree
With all that she confides to me.
And thus we travel, hand in hand,
The storied roads of Fairyland.

Ah, Little One, when years have fled,
And left their silver on my head,
And when the dimming eyes of age
With difficulty scan the page,
Perhaps *I'll* turn the tables then;

Perhaps *I'll* put the question, when
I borrow of your better sight—
"Please—will you read to me to-night?"

THE BREAKFAST FOOD FAMILY

John Spratt will eat no fat,
   Nor will he touch the lean;
He scorns to eat of any meat,
   He lives upon Foodine.

But Mrs. Spratt will none of that,
   Foodine she cannot eat;
Her special wish is for a dish
   Of Expurgated Wheat.

To William Spratt that food is flat
   On which his mater dotes.
His favorite feed—his special need—
   Is Eata Heapa Oats.

But sister Lil can't see how Will
   Can touch such tasteless food.
As breakfast fare it can't compare,
   She says, with Shredded Wood.

Now, none of these Leander please,
   He feeds upon Bath Mitts.
While sister Jane improves her brain
   With Cero-Grapo-Grits.

Lycurgus votes for Father's Oats;
   Proggine appeals to May;
The junior John subsists upon
   Uneeda Bayla Hay.

Corrected Wheat for little Pete;
   Flaked Pine for Dot; while "Bub"
The infant Spratt is waxing fat
   On Battle Creek Near-Grub.

"TREASURE ISLAND"

Comes little lady, a book in hand,
A light in her eyes that I understand,
And her cheeks aglow from the faery breeze
That sweeps across the uncharted seas.
She gives me the book, and her word of praise
A ton of critical thought outweighs.
"I've finished it, daddie!"—a sigh thereat.
"Are there any more books in the world like that?"

No, little lady. I grieve to say
That of all the books in the world to-day
There's not another that's quite the same
As this magic book with the magic name.
Volumes there be that are pure delight,
Ancient and yellowed or new and bright;
But—little and thin, or big and fat—
There are no more books in the world like that.

And what, little lady, would I not give
For the wonderful world in which you live!
What have I garnered one-half as true
As the tales Titania whispers you?
Ah, late we learn that the only truth
Was that which we found in the Book of Youth.
Profitless others, and stale, and flat;—
There are no more books in the world like that.

A BALLADE OF SPRING'S UNREST

Up in the woodland where Spring
Comes as a laggard, the breeze
Whispers the pines that the King,
Fallen, has yielded the keys
To his White Palace and flees
Northward o'er mountain and dale.
Speed then the hour that frees!
Ho, for the pack and the trail!

Northward my fancy takes wing,
Restless am I, ill at ease.

Pleasures the city can bring
Lose now their power to please.
Barren, all barren, are these,
Town life's a tedious tale;
That cup is drained to the lees—
Ho, for the pack and the trail!

Ho, for the morning I sling
Pack at my back, and with knees
Brushing a thoroughfare, fling
Into the green mysteries:
One with the birds and the bees,
One with the squirrel and quail,
Night, and the stream's melodies—
Ho, for the pack and the trail!

L'Envoi

Pictures and music and teas,
Theaters—books even—stale.
Ho, for the smell of the trees!
Ho, for the pack and the trail!

WHY?

Why, when the sun is gold,
    The weather fine,
The air (this phrase is old)
    Like Gascon wine;—

Why, when the leaves are red,
    And yellow, too,
And when (as has been said)
    The skies are blue;—

Why, when all things promote
    One's peace and joy,—
A joy that is (to quote)
    Without alloy;—

Why, when a man's well off,
    Happy and gay,

Why must he go play golf
And spoil his day!

THE RIME OF THE CLARK STREET CABLE

(Now happily extinct.)

Twas in a vault beneath the street,
    In the trench of the traction rope,
That I found a guy with a fishy eye
    And a think tank filled with dope.

His hair was matted, his face was black,
    And matted and black was he;
And I heard this wight in the vault recite,
    "In a singular minor key":

"Oh, I am the guy with the fishy eye
    And the think tank filled with dope.
My work is to watch the beautiful botch
    That's known as the Clark Street Rope.

"I pipes my eye as the rope goes by
    For every danger spot.
If I spies one out I gives a shout,
    And we puts in another knot.

"Them knots is all like brothers to me,
    And I loves 'em, one and all."
The muddy guy with the fishy eye
    A muddy tear let fall.

"There goes a knot we tied last week,
    There's one what we tied to-day;
And there's a patch was hard to reach,
    And caused six hours' delay.

"Two hundred seventy-nine, all told,
    And I knows their history;
And I'm most attached to a break we patched
    In the winter of 'eighty-three.

"For every time that knot comes round
    It sings out, 'Howdy, Bill!

We'll walk 'em home to-night, old man,
From here to the Ferris Wheel.

"'We'll walk 'em in the rush hours, Bill,
A swearing company,
As we've walked 'em, Bill, since I was tied,
In the winter of 'eighty-three.'"

The muddy guy with the fishy eye
Let fall another tear.
"Them knots is wife and child to me;
I've known 'em forty year.

"For I am the guy with the fishy eye
And the think tank filled with dope,
Whose work is to watch the lovely botch
That's known as the Clark Street Rope."

MISS LEGION

She is hotfoot after Cultyure,
She pursues it with a club.
She breathes a heavy atmosphere
Of literary flub.
No literary shrine so far
But she is there to kneel;
But—
Her favorite line of reading
Is O. Meredith's "Lucille."

Of course she's up on pictures—
Passes for a connoisseur.
On free days at the Institute
You'll always notice her.
She qualifies approval
Of a Titian or Corot;
But—
She throws a fit of rapture
When she comes to Bouguereau.

And when you talk of music,
She is Music's devotee.

She will tell you that Beethoven
Always makes her wish to pray;
And "dear old Bach!" His very name
She says, her ear enchants;
     But—
Her favorite piece is Weber's
"Invitation to the Dance."

A BALLADE OF DEATH AND TIME

I hold it truth with him who sweetly sings—
The weekly music of the *London Sphere*—
That deathless tomes the living present brings:
Great literature is with us year on year.
Books of the mighty dead, whom men revere,
Remind me I can make *my* books sublime.
But prithee, bay my brow while I am here:
Why do we always wait for Death and Time?

Shakespeare, great spirit, beat his mighty wings,
As I beat mine, for the occasion near.
He knew, as I, the worth of present things:
Great literature is with us year on year.
Methinks I meet across the gulf his clear
And tranquil eye; his calm reflections chime
With mine: "Why do we at the present fleer?
Why do we always wait for Death and Time?"

The reading world with acclamation rings
For my last book. It led the list at Weir,
Altoona, Rahway, Painted Post, Hot Springs:
Great literature is with us year on year.
The *Bookman* gives me a vociferous cheer.
Howells approves! I can no higher climb.

Bring then the laurel, crown my bright career.
Why do we always wait for Death and Time?

    L'Envoi

Critics, who pastward, ever pastward peer,
Great literature is with us year on year.
Trumpet my fame while I am in my prime.
Why do we always wait for Death and Time?

THE KAISER'S FAREWELL TO PRINCE HENRY

Aufwiedersehen, brother mine!
  Farewells will soon be kissed;
And ere you leave to breast the brine
  Give me once more your fist;

That mailéd fist, clenched high in air
  On many a foreign shore,
Enforcing coaling stations where
  No stations were before;

That fist, which weaker nations view
  As if 'twere Michael's own,
And which appals the heathen who
  Bow down to wood and stone.

But this trip no brass knuckles. Glove
  That heavy mailéd hand;
Your mission now is one of Love
  And Peace—you understand.

All that's American you'll praise;
  The Yank can do no wrong.
To use his own expressive phrase,
  Just "jolly him along."

Express surprise to find, the more
  Of Roosevelt you see,
How much I am like Theodore,
  And Theodore like me.

I am, in fact, (this might not be
  A bad thing to suggest,)
The Theodore of the East, and he
  The William of the West.

And, should you get a chance, find out—
  If anybody knows—

15

Exactly what it's all about,
 That Doctrine of Monroe's.

That's *entre nous*. My present plan
 You know as well as I:
Be just as Yankee as you can;
 If needs be, eat some pie.

Cut out the 'kraut, cut out Rhine wine,
 Cut out the Schützenfest,
The Sängerbund, the Turnverein,
 The Kommers, and the rest.

And if some fool society
 "Die Wacht am Rhein" should sing,
You sing "My Country, 'Tis of Thee"—
 The tune's "God Save the King."

To our own kindred in that land
 There's not much you need tell.
Just tell them that you saw me, and
 That I was looking well.

TO LILLIAN RUSSELL

(*A reminiscence of 18—.*)

Dear Lillian! (The "dear" one risks;
"Miss Russell" were a bit austerer)—
Do you remember Mr. Fiske's
 Dramatic Mirror

Back when—? (But we'll not count the years;
The way they've sped is most surprising.)
You were a trifle in arrears
 For advertising.

I brought the bill to your address;
I was the *Mirror's* bill collector—
In Thespian haunts a more or less
 Familiar spectre.

On that (to me) momentous day
You dwelt amid the city's clatter,

A few doors west of old Broadway;
    The street—no matter.

But while you have forgot the debt,
And him who called in line of duty,
He never, never shall forget
    Your wondrous beauty.

You were too fair for mortal speech,—
Enchanting, positively rippin';
You were some dream, and quelque peach,
    And beaucoup pippin.

Your "fight with Time" had not begun,
Nor any reason to promote it;
No beauty battles to be won.
    Beauty? You wrote it!

"A bill?" you murmured in distress,
"A bill?" (I still can hear you say it.)
"A bill from Mr. Fiske? Oh, yes …
    I'll call and pay it."

And he, the thrice-requited kid,
That such a goddess should address him,
Could only blush and paw his lid,
    And stammer, "Yes'm!"

Eheu! It seems a cycle since,
But still the nerve of memory tingles.
And here you're writing Beauty Hints,
    And I these jingles.

DORNRÖSCHEN

In the great hall of Castle Innocence,
Hedged round with thorns of maiden doubts and fears,—
Within, without, a silence grave, intense,—
Her soul lies sleeping through the rose-leaf years.

Hedged round with thorns of maiden doubts and fears;
And all save one the thither path shall miss.
Her soul lies sleeping through the rose-leaf years,
Waiting the Prince and his awakening kiss.

And all save one the thither path shall miss;
For one alone may thread the thorn defence.
Waiting the Prince and his awakening kiss,
A hush broods over Castle Innocence.

For one alone may thread the thorn defence,
Care free, heart free, and singing on his way.
A hush broods over Castle Innocence
One comes to wake;—but when—ah, who can say!

Care free, heart free, and singing on his way,
One comes all thorns of Fear and Doubt to dare.
One comes to wake! But when? Ah, who can say
The hour his light feet press the castle stair?

One comes all thorns of Fear and Doubt to dare!
Thorns with his coming into roses bloom.
The hour his light feet press the castle stair
The warders of the castle hall give room.

Thorns with his coming into roses bloom;
For him the flowers of Trust and Faith unfold.
The warders of the castle hall give room
Before the young Prince of the Heart of Gold.

For him the flowers of Trust and Faith unfold;
Till then the thorns of maiden doubts and fears.
Before the young Prince of the Heart of Gold
Her rose-soul slumbers through the tranquil years.

Till then the thorns of maiden doubts and fears.
Within, without, a silence grave, intense.
Her rose-soul slumbers through the tranquil years
In the great hall of Castle Innocence.

"FAREWELL!"

(Evoked by Calverley's "Forever.")

"Farewell!" Another gloomy word
  As ever into language crept.
'Tis often written, never heard
    Except

In playhouse. Ere the hero flits
(In handcuffs) from our pitying view,
"Farewell!" he murmurs, then exits
    R. U.

"Farewell!" is much too sighful for
An age that has not time to sigh.
We say, "I'll see you later," or
    "Good-bye!"

"Fare well" meant long ago, before
It crept tear-spattered into song,
"Safe voyage!" "Pleasant journey!" or
    "So long!"

But gone its cheery, old-time ring:
The poets made it rime with knell.
Joined, it became a dismal thing—
    "Farewell!"

"Farewell!" Into the lover's soul
You see fate plunge the cruel iron.
All poets use it. It's the whole
    Of Byron.

"I only feel—farewell!" said he;
And always tearful was the telling.
Lord Byron was eternally
    Farewelling.

"Farewell!" A dismal word, 'tis true.
(And why not tell the truth about it?)
But what on earth would poets do
    Without it!

REFORM IN OUR TOWN

There was a man in Our Town
    And Jimson was his name,
Who cried, "Our civic government
    Is honeycombed with shame."
He called us neighbors in and said,
    "By Graft we're overrun.

Let's have a general cleaning up,
  As other towns have done."

The citizens of Our Town
  Responded to the call;
Beneath the banner of Reform
  We gathered one and all.
We sent away for men expert
  In hunting civic sin,
To ask these practised gentlemen
  Just how we should begin.

The experts came to Our Town
  And told us how 'twas done.
"Begin with Gas and Traction,
  And half your fight is won.
Begin with Gas and Traction;
  The rest will follow soon."
We looked at one another
  And hummed a different tune.

Said Smith, "Saloons in Our Town
  Are palaces of shame."
Said Jones, "Police corruption
  Has hurt the town's fair name."
Said Brown, "Our lawless children
  Pitch pennies as they please."
Now would it not be wiser
  To start Reform with these?

The men who came to Our Town
  Replied, "No haste with these;
Begin with Gas—or Water—
  The roots of the disease."
We looked at one another
  And hemmed and hawed a bit;
Enthusiasm faded then
  From every single cit.

The men who came to Our Town
  Expressed a mild surprise,
Then they too at each other
  Looked "with a wild surmise."
Jimson had stock in Traction,
  And Jones had stock in Gas,

And Smith and Brown in this and that,
  So—nothing came to pass.

The profligates of Our Town
  Pitch pennies as of yore;
Police corruption flourishes
  As rankly as before,
Still are our gilded ginmills
  Foul palaces of shame.
Reform is just as distant
  As when the wise men came.

WHEN THE SIRUP'S ON THE FLAPJACK

When the sirup's on the flapjack and the coffee's in the pot;
When the fly is in the butter—where he'd rather be than not;
When the cloth is on the table, and the plates are on the cloth;
When the salt is in the shaker and the chicken's in the broth;
When the cream is in the pitcher and the pitcher's on the tray,
And the tray is on the sideboard when it isn't on the way;
When the rind is on the bacon and likewise upon the cheese,
Then I somehow feel inspired to do a string of rimes like these.

BREAD PUDDYNGE

When good King Arthur ruled our land
  He was a goodly king,
And his idea of what to eat
  Was a good bag puddynge.

The bag puddynge he had in mind
  Was thickly strewn with plums,
With alternating lumps of fat
  As big as my two thumbs.

"My love," quoth he to Guinevere,
  "We have a joust to-day—
Sir Launce is here, Sir Tris, Sir Gal,
  And all the brave array.

"Put everything across to-night
    In guise of goodly fare,
And cook us up a bag puddynge
    That will y-curl our hair."

"I'll curl your hair," said Guinevere,
    "As tight as tight can be;
I'll cook you up a bag puddynge
    From my new recipee."

"Pitch in and eat, my merry men!"
    That night the King did say;
"But save a little room—a bag
    Puddynge is on the way.

"Ho! here it comes! Now, by my sword,
    A famous feast 'twill be.
Queen Guinevere hath cooked it, Launce,
    From her own recipee."

"Odslife!" cried Launce, "if there is aught
    I love 'tis this same thing."
And he and all the knights did fall
    Upon that bag puddynge.

One taste, and every holy knight
    Sat speechless for a space,
While disappointment and disgust
    Were writ in every face.

"Odsbodikins!" Sir Tristram cried,
    "In all my days, by Jing!
I ne'er did taste so flat a mess
    As this here bag puddynge."

"Odswhiskers, Arthur!" cried Sir Launce,
    Whose license knew no bounds,
"I would to Godde I had this stuff
    To poultice up my wounds."

King Arthur spat his mouthful out,
    And sent for Guinevere.
"What is this frightful mess?" he roared.

"Is this a joke, my dear?"

"Oh, ain't it good?" asked Guinevere,
  Her face a rosy red.
"I thought 'twould make an awful hit:
  I made it out of bread!"

When good King Arthur ruled our land
  He was a goodly king,
And only once in all his reign
  Was made a Bread Puddynge.

MUSCA DOMESTICA

Baby bye, here's a fly,
We will watch him, you and I;
Lest he fall in Baby's mouth,
Bringing germs from north and south.
In the world of things a-wing
There is not a nastier thing
Than this pesky little fly;—
So we'll watch him, you and I.

See him crawl up the wall,
And he'll never, never fall;
Save that, poisoned, he may drop
In the soup or on the chop.
Let us coax the cunning brute
To the tempting Tanglefoot,
Or invite his thirsty soul
To the poison-paper bowl.

I believe with six such legs
You or I could walk on eggs;
But he'd rather crawl on meat
With his microbe-laden feet.
Eggs would hardly do as well—
He could not get through the shell;
Better far, to spread disease,

Vegetables, meat, or cheese.

There he goes, on his toes,
Tickling, tickling Baby's nose.
Heaven knows where he has been,
And what filth he's wallowed in.
Drat the nasty little wretch!
He's the deuce and all to ketch.
Ah! He's settled on the wall.
Now the thunderbolt shall fall!

Baby bye, see that fly?
We will swat him, you and I.

THE PASSIONATE PROFESSOR

> *"But bending low, I whisper only this:
> 'Love, it is night.'"*
> —HARRY THURSTON PECK.

Love, it is night. The orb of day
Has gone to hit the cosmic hay.
    Nocturnal voices now we hear.
    Come, heart's delight, the hour is near
When Passion's mandate we obey.

I would not, sweet, the fact convey
In any crude and obvious way:
    I merely whisper in your ear—
        "Love, it is night!"

Candor compels me, pet, to say
That years my fading charms betray.
    Tho' Love be blind, I grant it's clear
    I'm no Apollo Belvedere.
But after dark all cats are gray.
        Love, it is night!

A BALLADE OF WOOL-GATHERING

Now is my season of unrest,
Now calls the forest, day and night;
And by its pleasant spell obsessed,
My wits go soaring like a kite.
Forgive me if I be not bright,
And pardon if I seem distrait;
Wood-fancies put my wits to flight;—
The woods are but a week away.

Palleth upon my soul the jest,
Falleth upon my pen a blight.
The daily task has lost its zest,
And everything is flat and trite.
There's nothing humorous in sight;
Don't mind if I am dull to-day.
For every column is a fight
When woods are but a week away.

Woods in the robes of summer dressed—
In greens and grays and browns bedight!
A journey on a river's breast,
Beneath the wedded blue-and-white!...
This end the Voyage of Delight
Waits, in a little wood-bound bay,
A bark canoe, all trim and tight;—
The woods are but a week away!

L'Envoi

Dear Reader, there is much to write;
I've many weighty things to say.
But who can write when woods invite,
And woods are but a week away!

TO THE SUN

(Variations on a theme by Gilbert.)

Shine on, Old Top, shine on!
Across the realms of space
    Shine on!

What though I'm in a sorry case?
What though my collar is a wreck,
And hangs a rag about my neck?
What though at food I can but peck?
    Never *you* mind!
        Shine on!

Shine on, Old Top, shine on!
Through leagues of lifeless air
        Shine on!
It's true I've no more shirts to wear,
My underwear is soaked, 'tis true,
My gullet is a redhot flue—
But don't let that unsettle you!
    Never *you* mind!
        Shine on!   [*It shines on.*]

WHEN IT IS HOT

"And Nebuchadnezzar commanded the most mighty men that were in his army to bind Shadrach, Meshach, and Abed-nego, and to cast them into the burning fiery furnace."

Consider Mr. Shadrach,
    Of fiery furnace fame:
He didn't bleat about the heat
    Or fuss about the flame.
He didn't stew and worry,
    And get his nerves in kinks,
Nor fill his skin with limes and gin
    And other "cooling drinks."

Consider Mr. Meshach,
    Who felt the furnace too:
He let it sizz nor queried "Is
    It hot enough for you?"
He didn't mop his forehead,
    And hunt a shady spot;
Nor did he say, "Gee! what a day!
    Believe me, it's some hot."

Consider, too, Abed-nego,

Who shared his comrades' plight:
He didn't shake his coat and make
  Himself a holy sight.
He didn't wear suspenders
  Without a coat and vest;
Nor did he scowl and snort and howl,
  And make himself a pest.

Consider, friends, this trio—
  How little fuss they made.
They didn't curse when it was worse
  Than ninety in the shade.
They moved about serenely
  Within the furnace bright,
And soon forgot that it was hot,
  With "no relief in sight."

THE SIMPLE, HEARTFELT LAY

Lives of poets oft remind us
  Not to wait too long for Time,
But, departing, leave behind us
  Obvious facts embalmed in rime.

Poems that we have to ponder
  Turn us prematurely gray;
We are infinitely fonder
  Of the simple, heartfelt lay.

Whitman's *Leaves of Grass* is odious,
  Browning's *Ring and Book* a bore.
Bleat, O bards, in lines melodious,—
  Bleat that two and two is four!

Must we hunt for hidden treasures?
  Nay! We want the heartfelt straight.
Minstrel, sing, in obvious measures—
  Sing that four and four is eight!

Whitman leads to easy slumbers,
  Browning makes us hunt the hay.
Pipe, ye potes, in simplest numbers,

Anything ye have to say.

Q·HORATIVS·FLACCVS
B· L· T·SVO·SALVTEM

HAEC·CARMINA·MI·VETVLE·QVAE
ME·IVVENE·PARVM·DILIGENTER
COMPOSITA·EXCIDERVNT·SENEX
REFICIENDA·LIMANDAQVE·IAM
DVDVM·EXISTIMO·QVOD·NVNC
DEMVM·FACTVM·EST·MIRARIS
FORTASSE·CVR·ANGLICE·RE
SCRIPSERIM·DESINES·MIRARI
CVM·DIXERO·SINE·FVCO·OPOR
TERE·POETA·ETIAM·VIVVS·NON
SOLVM·ACCOMMODEM·MEA·OPERA
AD·NORMAM·RECENTIORVM·TEM
PORVM·SED·ETIAM·VTAR·NEMPE
EA·LINGVA·QVAE·MAIORE·RE
SILIENDI·VT·ITA·DICAM·VI
PRAEDITA·VIDEATVR·VELIM
SINT·NOVI·VERSVS·TIBI·MVL
TO·IVCVNDIORES·QVAM·PRIS
CA·EXEMPLA

SCRIBEBAM·HELNGON
XVII·KAL·DEC

A NOTE FROM MR. FLACCUS

(Concerning the verses that follow.)

Dear B. L. T.:

You know my "pomes." Well, old man, I was pretty young when I got them out of my system, and they seem rather raw to me now—I'm getting along, you know; so I've been thinking that I'd do 'em over again, file 'em down, as we used to say. Enclosed is the result of my labors.

I presume you are wondering why I have done them into United States; but you know perfectly well that a poet as much alive as I am to-day must not only keep up with the procession, but choose a thought-vehicle that has good springs to it—"beaucoup resiliency," I s'pose you'd call it.

I hope you will like these new lines of mine better than their prototypes.

Yours regardfully,
Q. H. F.
Helngon, November 15.

———

I

TO ARISTIUS FUSCUS

"Integer vitæ scelerisque purus."

Fuscus, old scout, if a guy's on the level
    That's all the arsenal he'll have to tote;
Up to St. Peter or down to the Devil,
    No need to carry a gun in his coat.

Prowling around, as you know is my habit,
    I met a wolf in the forest, and he
Beat it for Wolfville and ran like a rabbit.
    (He was some wolf, too, receive it from me.)

Where I may happen to camp is no matter,—
    Paris, Chicago, Ostend or St. Joe,—
Like the old dame in the nursery patter
    I shall make music wherever I go.

Drop me in Dawson or chuck me in Cadiz,
    Dump me in Kansas or plant me in Rome,—
I shall keep on making love to the ladies:
    Where there's a skirt is my notion of home.

II

DUETTO

"Donec gratus eram."

HORACE:

29

What time my Lydia owned me lord
    No Persian king had much on Horace;
And when you blew my bed and board
    I was some sad, believe me, Mawruss.

LYDIA:

What time you loved no other She,
    Before this Chloë person signed you,
I flourished like a green bay tree;
    Now I'm the Girl You Left Behind You.

HORACE:

This Chloë dame that takes my eye
    Has so peculiar an allurance
I would not hesitate to die
    If she could cop my life insurance.

LYDIA:

Well, as for that, I know a gent
    With whom it's some delight to dally.
With me he makes an awful dent;
    I'd perish once or twice for Cally.

HORACE:

Suppose our former love should go
    Into a new de luxe edition?
Suppose I tie a can to Chlo,
    And let you play your old position?

LYDIA:

Why, then, you cork, you butterfly,
    You sweet, philandering, perjured villain,
With you I'd love to live and die,
    Tho' Cally boy were twice as killin'.

III

TO PYRRHA

> *"Quis multa gracilis."*

What young tin whistle gent,
Bedaubed with barber's scent,—
    What cheapskate waits on you
    To woo,

O Pyrrha?

For whom the puff and rat
And transformation that
    You bought a year ago
    Or so,
        O Pyrrha?

Peeved? Not a bit. Not I
I'm sorry for the guy.
    He draws a lovely lime
    This time,
        O Pyrrha!

I've dipped. The wet ain't fine.
Hung on the votive line
    My duds. The gods can see
    I'm free.
        Eh, Pyrrha!

IV

TO ARISTIUS FUSCUS

"My sweetly-smiling, sweetly-speaking Lalage."

Fuscus, take a tip from me:
    This here job's no bed of roses,
Not the cinch it seems to be,
    Not the pipe that one supposes.
        What care I, tho', if I may
        Lallygag with Lalage.

Every day there's ink to spill,
    Tho' I may not feel like working.
Every day a hole to fill;
    One must plug it—there's no shirking.
        Oh, that I might all the day
        Lallygag with Lalage!

People say, "Gee! what a snap,
    Turning paragraphs and verses.
He's the band on Fortune's cap,
    Gets a barrel of ses-*terces*."
        Let them gossip, while I play

Hide and seek with Lalage.

People hand me out advice:
  "Hod, you're doing too much drivel.
Write us something sweet and nice.
  Stow the satire, chop the frivol."
    But we have the rent to pay,
    Lalage; eh, Lalage?

Ladies shy the saving sense
  Write me patronizing letters;
And there are the writing gents,
  Always out to knock their betters.
    What cares Flaccus if he may
    Lallygag with Lalage!

No, old top, the writing lay's
  Not a bed of sweet geranium.
Brickbats mingle with bouquets
  Shied at my devoted cranium.
    Does it peeve yours truly? Nay.
    Nothing can—with Lalage.

Paste this, Fuscus, in your hat:
  Not a pesky thing can peeve me.
Take it, too, from Horace flat,
  She's some gal, is Lal, believe me.
    So I coin this word to-day,
    "Lallygag"—from Lalage.

V

TO SYLVIA

Were I on the Latin lay,
Were I turning Odes to-day,
You would draw a gem from me,
Little maid of mystery!

In an Ode I'd love to spout you;
I am simply bug about you.
That's the way!—the fairest peach
Is the one that's out of reach.

I have toasted in my time

Many a peach (and many a lime),
All of them, I must confess,
Lacking your elusiveness.

Lalage, my well known flame,
Was considerable dame;
Likewise Lydia and Phyllis,
Chloë, Pyrrha, Amaryllis.

Syl, if you had lived when they did
You'd have had those damsels faded.
(That will give you, girl, some notion
Of your Flaccus's devotion.)

Yep. If I were doing Odes
In my quondam favorite modes,
With your image to qui-vive me
I'd tear off some Ode, believeme!

————————————————

A BALLAD OF MISFITS

"Chacun son métier:
Les vaches seront bien gardées."
—La Fontaine.

With skill for doing this or that
    The Lord each man endows.
Some men are best for pushing pens,
    And some for pushing plows;
And oh, the many many more
    That should be tending cows!
        Chacun son métier:
        Les vaches bien gardées.

The ivory-headed serving maid
    Who poses as a "cook,"
She hath a very bovine brain,
    She hath a bovine look.
Oh, prithee, lead her to the kine,
    Oh, prithee get the hook!
        Chacun son métier:
        Les vaches bien gardées.

The papering-and-painting gents
  Whose work is never done,
Who mess around your house until
  You pine to pull a gun,
Who take three mortal days to do
  What should be done in one;—
    Chacun son métier:
    Les vaches bien gardées.

The pestilential "pianiste,"
  The screechy singer too,
The writer of the stupid book
  And of the dull review,
The actor who is greatest when
  He takes his exit cue;—
    Chacun son métier:
    Les vaches bien gardées.

If every one were set to do
  The task for which he's fit,
The writer of these trifling lines
  Might also have to quit.
At tending cows the undersigned
  Might make an awful hit.
    Chacun son métier:
    Les vaches bien gardées.

AN ORIENTAL APOLOGY

When the hour was come Prince Chun arose,
And balanced a shoestring on his nose.
"From this some notion you will get,"
Said he, "of China's deep regret."

Now balancing upon his ear
A stein of foaming lager beer,
"This attitude," said he, "reveals
How very sorry China feels."

Then spinning top-like on his cue,
"I can't begin to tell to you
The deep remorse we suffer for

The death of your Ambassador."

Next, placing on his cue a plate,
He said, as it 'gan to gyrate:
"Nothing that's happened in his reign
Has caused my Emperor so much pain."

Upon his back he did declare,
While juggling five balls in the air,
"This attitude—the humblest yet—
Expresses personal regret."

Last, spreading out a deck of cards—
"Accept my Emperor's regards.
As our intentions were well meant,
Pray overlook the incident."

THE DAY OF THE COMET

(*May 18, 1910.*)

Here it is—Eighteenth of May!
Dawneth now the fatal day
When we take the awful veil
Of the fearsome comet's tail.
        Vale, Earth!

What will happen, heaven knows;
We can't even guess, suppose,
Hazard, speculate, surmise,
Hint, conjecture, theorize,
        Or divine.

Will we merely drill a hole
Through the trailing aureole?
Or will the prediction dire
Of a world destroyed by fire
        Be fulfilled?

Shall we crook our knees and pray
Counting this the Judgment Day?
Or preserve a cosmic ca'm,
Caring not a cosmic dam
        What may come?

There's the rub. If we but knew
We should know just what to do.
Yes is just as good as No
To all questions. Here we go!—
     Hang on tight!

THE MORNING AFTER

     (*May 19, 1910.*)

Here we are, friends, whole and hale
In or through the comet's tail;
And as far as we can say,
Matters are about as they
     Were before.

Everything is much the same
As before the comet came.
Grasses grow and waters run—
Nothing new beneath the sun—
     Same old sphere.

Life is drab or life is gay,
Thorny path or primrose way;
All is common, all is strange;
"Down the ringing grooves of change"
     Spins the world.

Change but of a humdrum kind.
What we vaguely had in mind
Was some new sensation or
Thrill we never felt before.
     Vain desire!

Nothing's added to the stock:
Same old shiver, same old shock.
Round about the sun we'll go
In the same old status quo.
     Awful bore!

A BALLADE OF IRRESOLUTION

Isolde, in the story old,
When Ireland's coast the vessel nears,
And Death were fairer to behold,
To Tristan gives "the cup that clears."
Straight to their fate the helmsman steers:
Unknowing, each the potion sips....
Comes echoing through the ghostly years
"Give me the philtre of thy lips!"

Ah, that like Tristan I were bold!
My soul into the future peers,
And passion flags, and heart grows cold,
And sicklied resolution veers.
I see the Sister of the Shears
Who sits fore'er and snips, and snips....
Still falls upon my inward ears,
"Give me the philtre of thy lips!"

Hero of lovers, largely soul'd!
Imagination thee enspheres
With song-enchanted wood and wold
And casements fronting magic meres.
Tristan, thy large example cheers
The faint of heart; thy story grips!—
My soul again that echo hears,
"Give me the philtre of thy lips!"

L'Envoi

Sweet sorceress, resolve my fears!
He stakes all who Elysium clips.
What tho' the fruit be tares and tears!—
Give me the philtre of thy lips!

TO WHAT BASE USES!

"Mrs. O—— now takes her daily dip at 5 in the afternoon, instead of in the morning."
                    —Newport Item.

37

This is the forest primeval.

This the spruce with the glorious plume
That grew in the forest primeval.

This is the lumberman big and browned
Who felled the spruce tree to the ground
That grew in the forest primeval.

This is the man with the paper mill
Who bought the pulp that paid the bill
Of the husky lumberjack who chopped
The lofty spruce and its branches lopped
That grew in the forest primeval.

This is the publisher bland and rich
Who bought the roll of paper which
Was made by the man with the paper mill
Who bought the pulp that paid the bill
Of the lumberjack with the murderous ax
Who felled the spruce with lusty hacks
That grew in the forest primeval.

This is the youth with the writing tool
Who does the daily Newport drool
That helps to make the publisher rich
Who ordered the stock of paper which
Was made by the man with the paper mill
Who bought the pulp that paid the bill
Of the husky Swede in the Joseph's coat
Who swung his ax and the tall spruce smote
That grew in the forest primeval.

This is the lady far from slim
Who changed the hour of her daily swim
And excited the youth with the writing tool
Who does the Newport drivel and drool
For the prosperous publisher bland and fat
Who ordered the virgin paper that
Was made by the man with the paper mill
Who bought the pulp that paid the bill
Of Ole Oleson the husky Swede
Who did a foul and darksome deed
When he swung his ax with vigor and vim
And smote the spruce tree tall and trim

That grew in the forest primeval.

This is the shop girl Mag or Liz
Who daily devours what news there is
Concerning the lady far from slim
Who changed the time of her ocean swim
And excited the youth with the writing tool
Who does the daily Newport drool
For the pursy publisher bland and rich
Who bought the innocent paper which
Was made by the man with the paper mill
Who bought the pulp that paid the bill
Of the Swedish jack who slew the spruce
That came to a most ignoble use—
The lofty spruce with the glorious plume—
The giant spruce that used to loom
In the heart of the forest primeval.

HOW THEY MIGHT HAVE BROUGHT THE GOOD NEWS

We sprang to the motor, I, Joris and Dirck.
I snapped on my goggles and got to my work.
"Hi, there!" yelled the cop in the helmet of white;
"Let her flicker!" said Joris, and into the night,
With a sneer at the speed laws, we hurtled hell-bent
To carry to Aix the good tidings from Ghent.

The going was poor, we expected delay,
And the usual livestock obstructed the way.
At Boom we ran over a large yellow dog,
At Düffeld a chicken, at Mecheln a hog;
What else, we'd no time to slow down to inquire;
At Aerschot, confound it! we blew out a tire.

I jacked up the axle and ripped off the shoe,
And snapped on an extra that promised to do.
"All aboard!" I exclaimed as I cranked the machine,
But something was wrong with the curst gasoline.
"By Hasselt!" Dirck groaned, "We'll be half a day late;
We ought to have sent the good tidings by freight."

False prophet! I tinkered a minute or two

And again we were off like "a bolt from the blue."
We ate up the hills at a forty-mile clip,
And skidded the turns like the snap of a whip,
Till we dashed into Aix and were pinched by a cop
For failing to slow when commanded to stop.

"Now, wouldn't that frost you!" said Joris, but we
When we told the glad tidings were instantly free.
The Mayor himself paid the ten dollars' fine,
And blew us to dinner with six kinds of wine,
Which (the burgesses voted, by common consent)
Was no more than their due that brought good news from Ghent.

THE DINOSAUR

Behold the mighty Dinosaur,
Famous in prehistoric lore,
Not only for his weight and strength
But for his intellectual length.
You will observe by these remains
The creature had two sets of brains—
One in his head (the usual place),
The other at his spinal base.
Thus he could reason *a priori*
As well as *a posteriori*.
No problem bothered him a bit;
He made both head and tail of it.
So wise he was, so wise and solemn,
Each thought filled just a spinal column.
If one brain found the pressure strong
It passed a few ideas along;
If something slipped his forward mind
'Twas rescued by the one behind;
And if in error he was caught
He had a saving afterthought.
As he thought twice before he spoke
He had no judgments to revoke;
For he could think, without congestion,
Upon both sides of every question.

Oh, gaze upon this model beast,

Defunct ten million years at least.

A BALLADE OF CAP AND BELLS

When as a dewdrop joy enspheres
This pleasant planet, arched with blue,
When every prospect charms and cheers,
And all the world is fair to view—
Who does not envy (have not you?)
That mortal, by Thalia kissed,
Who plies, in plumes of cockatoo,
The blithesome trade of humorist?

But when the wind of fortune veers,
And blue-white skies turn leaden hue,
When every pleasant prospect blears
And all the weary world's askew—
Who then would envy (if he knew)
Jack Point the jester, glum and trist;
Or ply, tho' first of all the crew,
The dismal trade of humorist?

Ah, jocund trifles writ in tears,
And merry stanzas steeped in rue!
When all the world in drab appears
The fool must still in motley woo.
Tho' bitter be the cud he chew,
Still must he grind his foolish grist;
Still must he ply, the long day through,
The tragic trade of humorist!

L'Envoi

Lady of Tears, what pains perdue
The heart and soul of him may twist
Who doth in cap and bells pursue
The glad sad trade of humorist!

41

GENTLE DOCTOR BROWN

It was a gentle sawbones and his name was Doctor Brown.
His auto was the terror of a small suburban town.
His practice, quite amazing for so trivial a place,
Consisted of the victims of his homicidal pace.

So constant was his practice and so high his motor's gear
That at knocking down pedestrians he never had a peer;
But it must, in simple justice, be as truly written down
That no man could be more thoughtful than gentle Doctor Brown.

Whatever was the errand on which Doctor Brown was bent
He'd stop to patch a victim up and never charged a cent.
He'd always pause, whoever 'twas he happened to run down:
A humane and a thoughtful man was gentle Doctor Brown.

"How fortunate," he would observe, "how fortunate 'twas I
That knocked you galley-west and heard your wild and wailing cry.
There *are* some heartless wretches who would leave you here alone,
Without a sympathetic ear to catch your dying moan.

"Such callousness," said Doctor Brown, "I cannot comprehend;
To fathom such indifference I simply don't pretend.
One ought to do his duty, and I never am remiss.
A simple word of thanks is all I ask. Here, swallow this!"

Then, reaching in the tonneau, he'd unpack his little kit,
And perform an operation that was workmanlike and fit.
"You may survive," said Doctor Brown; "it's happened once or twice.
If not, you've had the benefit of competent advice."

Oh, if all our motormaniacs were equally humane,
How little bitterness there'd be, or reason to complain!
How different our point of view if we were ridden down
By lunatics as thoughtful as gentle Doctor Brown!

IN THE GALLERY

Weirder than the pictures
Are the folks who come
With their owlish strictures—
Telling why they're bum.
Of all lines of babble

This one has the call:
Picture gallery gabble
Is the best of all.

Literary fluffle
Never, never cloys;
Much has Mrs. Guffle
Added to my joys.
For that chitter-chatter
I delight to fall.
But the picture patter
Is the best of all.

With the music highbrows
I delight to chat,
Elevating my brows
Over this and that.
Music tittle-tattle
Never fails to thrall.
But the picture prattle
Is the best of all.

Sociologic rub-dub
I delight to hear;
Philosophic flub-dub
Titillates my ear.
Lovelier yet the spiffle
In the picture hall;
For the picture piffle
Is the best of all.

Weirder than the pictures
Are the folks who stand
Passing owlish strictures,
Catalogue in hand.
Hear the bunk they babble
Under every wall.
Yes. The gallery gabble
Is the best of all.

ALWAYS

"Il y a tous les jours quelque dam chose."
—ABELARD TO HELOISE.

When Mrs. Mead was full of groans,
    When symptoms of all sorts assailed her,
She sent for bluff old Doctor Jones,
    And told him all the things that ailed her.
It took her nearly half the day,
    And when she finished out the string—
"Ye-e-s, Mrs. Mead," drawled Doctor J.,
    "There's always some dam thing."

I like the line. It's worth a ton
    Of optimistic commonplaces.
It's tonic, it refreshes one,
    It cheers, it stimulates, it braces.
It summarizes things so well;
    It has the philosophic ring.
Has Kant or Hegel more to tell?
    "There's always some dam thing."

The dean of all the cheer-up school
    Adjures sad hearts to cease repining,
And intimates that, as a rule,
    The sun behind the cloud is shining.
"Into each life——" You know the rest;
    No need to finish out the string.
Longfellow boiled might be expressed,
    "There's always some dam thing."

When things go wrong I do not read
    The cheer-up poets, great or lesser.
To soothe my soul I do not need
    The Neo-Thought of Mr. Dresser.
Sufficient for each working day,
    With all the worries it may bring,
That helpful line by Doctor J.,
    "There's always some dam thing."

THE MODERN MARINER

A dry sheet and a lazy sea,

And a wind so far from fast
It barely floats the owner's flag
   That flutters at the mast—
That flutters at the mast, my boys;
   So while the sky is free
Of cloud we'll take a yachtsman's chance
   And venture out to sea.

The aneroid has dropped a tenth!
   Back, back across the bar
To a harbor snug, and a long cold drink,
   And a big fat black cigar—
A big fat black cigar, my boys;
   While, on an even keel,
The Swedish chef out-chefs himself
   In getting up a meal.

Give me a soft and gentle wind,
   A fleckless azure sky;
I care not for your "snoring breeze"
   And dinners heaving high—
And dinners heaving high, my boys,
   Make no great hit with me;
So when the breeze begins to snore
   We'll not put out to sea.

There's laughter in yon beach hotel,
   And summer girls a crowd;
And hark the music, mariners,
   The band is piping loud!
The band is piping loud, my boys,
   Bright eyes are flashing free.
Come, fly the owner's-absent flag
   And join the revelry.

A BALLADE OF THE CANNERY

What of the phrases, long decayed,
Of paleologic pedigree,
Musty, moldy, frazzled, and frayed—
A doddering, dusty company?

What shall be done with them? say we;
And east and west the people bawl,
Dump them into the Cannery!—
Into the brine go one and all.

"Grilled" and "lauded" and "scored" and "flayed,"
"Common or garden variety,"
"Wave of crime" and "reform crusade,"
"Along these lines" and "it seems to me,"
"Noted savant," "I fail to see,"
The "groaning board" of the "banquet hall,"—
Masonjar 'em in "ghoulish glee"—
Into the brine go one and all.

"Succulent bivalves," "trusty blade,"
"Last analysis," "practical-ly,"
"Lone highwayman" and "fusillade,"
"Millionaire broker and clubman," "gee!"
"In reply to yours," "can such things be?"
"Sounded the keynote" or "trumpet call,"—
Can 'em, pickle 'em, one, two, three—
Into the brine go one and all.

L'Envoi

Under the spreading chestnut tree
Stands the Cannery, all too small.
The Canner a briny man is he,
And into the brine go one and all.

PANDEAN PIPEDREAMS

(Induced by smoking "Pagan Pickings.")

I

This is something that I heard,
As the fluting of a bird,
On a certain drowsy day,
When my pipe was under way.
I was weary of the town,
And the going up and down;

Sick of streets and sick of noise,—
And I pined for Pagan joys.

Daphne, here it is July!
Just the month, my love, to fly
To a sylvan solitude
In the green and ancient wood.
We will trip it as we go
On the neo-Pagan toe,
Sunny days and starry nights,
Savoring the wild delights
Of a turbulent desire
That may set the wood on fire.

We will play at hunt-the-fawn,
In the neo-Dorian dawn.
You will scamper through the brake,
And I'll follow in your wake—

As the young Apollo ran
In the piping days of Pan.
You'll escape me, without doubt,
For I'm just a trifle stout;
But, when I have lagged behind,
Waiting for my second wynde,
From some pretty hiding-place
Will emerge your laughing face;
I shall glimpse your eyes of blue,
Hear your merry "Peek-a-boo!"

What to wear? The Pagan plan
Contemplates a coat of tan;
But I fear we shall require
Just a trifle more attire.
Bushes scratch and brambles sting;
Insect myriads are a-wing;—
Heavens, how mosquitoes swarm
When the woodland air is warm.
(MEM: To take, when we elope,
Tanglewood Mosquito Dope.)

Do you like the picture, dear?
Have you aught of doubt or fear?
Have you any criticism
Of my neo-Paganism?

If not, dearie, let us fly
To that passion-ripening sky,
Where our souls may have their fling,
And our every care take wing.

So the bird song fluted by,
Like a vagrant summer sigh—
Came, and passed, and was no more;
And my pleasant dream was o'er.
For arose the wraith of Doubt;
And I knew my pipe was out.

II

This is something that befell
When my pipe was drawing well—
Something, rather, that I heard
As the fluting of a bird.

Daphne, come and live with me
In a Pagan greenery.
Life will then be naught but play,
One long Pagan holiday.
We will play at hide and seek
In the alders by the creek;
Sport amid the cascade's smother.
Splashing water at each other;—
Every moment pleasure wooing,
Every moment something doing.
If we talk, we'll talk of Love:
All its arguments we'll prove.
Such a mental rest you'll find.
Leave your intellect behind.

Night will come, (for come it will,
'Spite the fluting on the hill,)
And we'll pitch a cozy camp
Where it isn't quite so damp.
While you dry your hair and laze
By the campfire's violet blaze,
I will rob a balsam tree
To construct a house for thee.
What so dear as to be wooed

In a sylvan solitude?

What so sweet as Pagan vows
Whispered in a house of boughs?
Pagan love's without alloy.
Pagan kisses never cloy.
Arms that cling in Pagan fashion
Never tire. A Pagan passion
Is the only kind I know
That outlives a winter's snow.
Daphne, Daphne, let us fly!
You're a Pagan—so am I.

So the fluting on the hill
Passed and died, and all was still.
So the Pagan Pickings died,
And I laid the pipe aside.

THE LAUNDRY OF LIFE

(An Adventure in Sentiment.)

Life is a laundry in which we
Are ironed out, or soon or late.
Who has not known the irony
       Of fate?

We enter it when we are born,
Our colors bright. Full soon they fade.
We leave it "done up," old and worn,
       And frayed;

Frayed round the edges, worn and thin—
Life is a rough old linen slinger.
Who has not lost a button in
       Life's wringer?

With other linen we are tubbed,
With other linen often tangled;
In open court we then are scrubbed,
       And mangled.

Some take a gloss of happiness
The hardest wear can not diminish;

Others, alas! get a "domes-
    Tic finish."

WISDOM IN A CAPSULE

"If she be not so to me.
What care I how fair she be?"
        —THE SHEPHERD'S RESOLUTION.

Here we have in this truism
Mr. James's pragmatism.
Test your troubles day by day
With it, and they fly away.
Is the weather boiling hot,
Hot enough to boil a pot—
If it be not so to me,
What care I how hot it be?

Take a pudding made of bread;
Much against it has been said;
But it does not lack defense—
Many say it is immense.
Be it damned or be it blessed,
Let us make the acid test—
If it be not so to me,
What care I how good it be?

So with every blooming thing
That has power to soothe or sting;
Ships or shoes or sealing wax,
Carrots, comets, carpet tacks.
Every philosophic need
Covered by this capsule creed:
If it be not so to me,
What care I how ${good \atop bad}$ it be?

THE LAND OF RAINBOW'S-END

Young Faintheart lay on a wayside bank,

50

Full prey to doubts and fears,
When he did espy come trudging by
    A Pilgrim bent with years.
His back was bowed and his step was slow,
    But his faith no years could bend,
As he eagerly pressed to the rose-lit west
    And the Land of Rainbow's-End.

"It's ho, for a pack!" sang the Pilgrim gray,
    "And a stout oak staff for friend,
And it's over the hills and far away
    To the Land of Rainbow's-End!"

"Thou'rt old," young Faintheart cried, "thou'rt old,
    And there's many a league to go;
And still thou seekest the pot of gold
    At the farther end of the bow."
"I am old, I am old," said the Pilgrim gray,
    "But ever my way I'll wend
To the rose-lit hills of the dying day
    And the Land of Rainbow's-End."

"Come, rest thee, rest thee by my side;
    Give o'er thy doomsday quest."
"Have done, have done!" the Pilgrim cried:
    "The light wanes in the west.
The road is long, but I shall not tire;
    I will lay my bones, God send,
By the beautiful City of Heart's Desire,
    In the Land of Rainbow's-End."

"Then it's ho, for a pack!" sang the Pilgrim gray,
    "And a stout oak staff for friend,
And it's over the hills and far away
    To the Land of Rainbow's-End."

A BALLADE OF A BORE

When the weather is warm and the glass running high
And the odors of Araby tincture the air;
When the sun is aloft in a white and blue sky,
And the morrow holds promise of falling as fair;—

In spring or in summer I'm free to declare,
And the same I am equally free to maintain,
One person has power my peace to impair:
The man who tells limericks gives me a pain.

When the foliage flushes and summer is by,
And russet and red are the popular wear;
When the song of the woodland is changed to a sigh
And the horn of the hunter is heard by the hare;—
In the season of autumn I'm free to declare,
And my language is lucid and simple and plain,
One person's acquaintance I freely forswear:
The man with the limerick gives me a pain.

When the landscape is iced and the snow feathers fly,
When the fields are all bald and the trees are all bare,
And the prospect which nature presents to the eye
Is chiefly distinguished by glitter and glare;—
In the season of winter I'm free to declare
That the limerick person is flat and inane.
This person, I think, we could easily spare:
The man who tells limericks gives me a pain.

L'Envoi

From New Year to Christmas I'm free to declare
That, for ways that are dull and for verse that is vain,
One bore is peculiar—and not at all rare:
The man with the limerick gives me a pain.

THE POLE

(*Tune*: "*Carcassonne.*")

I'm an old man, I'm eighty-three,
  I seldom get away;
My work, it keeps me close at home—
  I have no time for play.
If it were not for the journey back,
  That so fatigues a soul,
I'd like to take a little trip—

I never have seen the Pole.

'Tis said that in that favored place
    There is no heat or drouth;
And that, whichever way you turn,
    You're looking south-by-south.
Some say there is a flagstaff there,
    Some say there is a hole.
Think of the years that I have lived
    And never have seen the Pole!

The parson a hundred times is right—
    We ought to stay at home.
I'm an old man, I'm eighty-three,
    I have no call to roam.
And yet if I could somehow find
    The time—God bless my soul!—
I think that I would die content
    If I only could see the Pole!

My brother has seen Baraboo,
    If so he speak the truth;
My wife and son they both have been
    As far as to Duluth;
My cousin cruised to Eastport, Maine,
    On a ship that carried coal;
I've been as far as Mackinac—
    But I never have seen the Pole!

SH-H-H-H!

"Mr. Mabie is now reading the summer books."
—THE LADIES' HOME JOURNAL.

What shall we buy for a summer's day?
What is good reading and what is not?
Mabie will tell us—we wait his say;
For Mabie alone can know what's what.
Meanwhile the world is as still as death;
Mute inquiry is in men's looks;
Everybody is holding his breath—
Mabie is reading the summer books.

The suns are at pause in the cosmic race;
The mills of the gods have ceased to grind;
The only sound that is heard in space
Is the rhythmic clicking of Mabie's mind.
Elsewhere silence, or near or far—
Chattering Pleiads or babbling brooks;
For the whisper has passed from star to star:
"Mabie is reading the summer books."

THE VANISHED FAY

Tell me, whither do they go,
All the Little Ones we know?
They "grow up" before our eyes,
And the fairy spirit flies.
Time the Piper, pied and gay—
Does he lure them all away?
Do they follow after him,
Over the horizon's brim?

Daughter's growing fair to see,
Slim and straight as popple tree.
Still a child in heart and head,
But—the fairy spirit's fled.
As a fay at break of day,
Little One has flown away,
On the stroke of fairy bell—
When and whither, who can tell?

Still her childish fancies weave
In the Land of Make Believe;
And her love of magic lore
Is as avid as before.
Dollies big and dollies small
Still are at her beck and call.
But for all this pleasant play,
Little One has gone away.

Whither, whither have they flown,
All the fays we all have known?
To what "faery lands forlorn"

On the sound of elfin horn?
As she were a woodland sprite,
Little One has vanished quite.
Waves the wand of Oberon:
Cock has crowed—the fay is gone!

AUTUMN REVERY

When the leaves are falling crimson
    And the worm is off its feed,
When the rag weed and the jimson
    Have agreed to go to seed,
When the air in forest bowers
    Has a tang like Rhenish wine,
And to breathe it for two hours
    Makes you feel you'd like to dine,
When the frost is on the pumpkin
    And the corn is in the shock,
And the cheek of country bumpkin
    City faces seems to mock,—
When you come across a ditty
    (Like this one) of Autumn's charm,
Then it's pleasant in the city,
    Where they keep the houses warm.

THE RECOIL

I met a friend of lofty brow—
As lofty as the laws allow.
I said to him, "You'll know, I'm sure—
What's doing now in litrychoor?"
Said he: "I hate the very name;
I'm weary of the blooming game.
I read, whenever I have time,
Something by Phillips Oppenheim."

"Cheer up!" said I. "What's new in Art?—
You drift around the picture mart.

What do you think of Mr. Blum?—
Some say he's great, some say he's bum."
"I'm strong for Blum," my friend replied;
"His pictures are so queer and pied.
I wouldn't change them if I could;
I'd rather have things queer than good."

I spoke of this, I spoke of that,
But everything was stale and flat.
Said I, "You once adored the chaste,
You used to have such perfect taste."
"Good taste," he wailed, "brings but distress,
'Tis an affliction, nothing less;
While those whose taste is punk and vile
Are happy all the blessed while."

"Oh, take a brace, old man!" said I.
"Let me prescribe a nip of rye,
And then we'll go to see a play;
I've two for Barrymore to-day."
"No, no," he groaned; "'twould be a bore,
With all respect to Barrymore."
Said I: "Then whither shall we go?"
Said he: "A moving picture show."

THE CORONATION

Lang Syne.

Twas a holy mystery
In the days of chivalry.
More than pageant was the Rite
In the sight of clod and knight.
Sword and Scepter, Orb and Rod,
Faith in self and faith in God;
Oaths of Homage fiercely flung,
Faith in heart and faith in tongue;—
    Gone the things that meaning gave
    "With the old world to the grave."

1911.

Knightly faith was born to fade:
Now the Rite is masquerade.
Now a cockney paladin
Winds a penny horn of tin.
Where in reverence heads were bowed
Surges now a careless crowd;
"Muddied oafs" and "flanneled fools"
Jostle "Yanks" with camping stools;—
  Gone the things that meaning gave
  "With the old world to the grave."

SONS OF BATTLE

Let us have peace, and Thy blessing,
  Lord of the Wind and the Rain,
When we shall cease from oppressing,
  From all injustice refrain;
When we hate falsehood and spurn it;
  When we are men among men.
Let us have peace when we earn it—
  Never an hour till then.

Let us have rest in Thy garden,
  Lord of the Rock and the Green,
When there is nothing to pardon,
  When we are whitened and clean.
Purge us of skulking and treason,
  Help us to put them away.
We shall have rest in Thy season;
  Till then the heat of the fray.

Let us have peace in Thy pleasure,
  Lord of the Cloud and the Sun;
Grant to us æons of leisure
  When the long battle is done.
Now we have only begun it;
  Stead us!—we ask nothing more.
Peace—rest—but not till we've won it—
  Never an hour before.

MY LADY NEW YORK

O siren of tresses peroxide,
    And heart that is hard as a flint,
Blue orbs of complacency ox-eyed,
    That light at the mark of the mint,
Ears only for jingle of joybells,
    A conscience as light as a cork—
You are wedded to follies and foibles,
    My Lady New York.

True, you have (not enough, tho', to hurt you)
    Your moods and your manners austere;
You have visions and vapors of virtue,
    And "reform" for a time has your ear;
But of chaste Puritanic embraces
    You soon have enough and to spare,
And then you kick over the traces,
    And virtue forswear.

So go it, milady! Foot fleetly
    The paths that are primrose and gay;
Abandon your fancy completely
    To follies and fads of the day.
"Reform" is a something that throttles
    The joys of the pace that's intense—
Smash hearts, reputations, and bottles,
    And ding the expense!

BALLADE OF THE PIPESMOKE CARRY

The Ancient Wood is white and still,
Over the pines the bleak wind blows,
Voiceless the brook and mute the rill,
Silence too where the river flows.
Still I catch the scent of the rose
And hear the white-throat's roundelay,
Footing the trail that Memory knows,
Over the hills and far away.

I have only a pipe to fill:
Weaving, wreathing rings disclose
A trail that flings straight up the hill,
Straight as an arrow's flight. For those
Who fare by night the pole star glows
Above the mountain top. By day
A blasted pine the pathway shows
Over the hills and far away.

The Ancient Wood is white and chill,
But what know I of wintry woes?
The Pipesmoke Trail is mine at will—
Naught may hinder and none oppose.
Such the power the pipe bestows,
When the wilderness calls I may
Tramping go, as I smoke and doze,
Over the hills and far away.

L'Envoi

Deep in the canyons lie the snows:
They shall vanish if I but say—
If my fancy a-roving goes
Over the hills and far away.

———————————————————————

POST-VACATIONAL

You have heard that mildewed story,
That tradition horned and hoary,
    That it wearies one to roam,
        Past a doubt;
That one vainly on vacation
Tries to find recuperation,
    Till he hunts his happy home
        Tuckered out.

That abroad there is no comfort,
That a man must journey home for 't—
    You have heard that whiskered wheeze,
        Have you not?

'Tis a commonplace to cavil
At the "luxuries of travel,"
   For in travel lack of ease
      Is your lot.

You have heard that gag historic;
It was often sprung by Yorick;
   It's as old as Noah's ark
      And its crew.
It's the commonest (at basis)
Of all common commonplaces;—
   So I merely would remark
      That—it's true.

THE BARDS WE QUOTE

Whene'er I quote I seldom take
From bards whom angel hosts environ;
But usually some damned rake
      Like Byron.

Of Whittier I think a lot,
My fancy to him often turns;
But when I quote 'tis some such sot
      As Burns.

I'm very fond of Bryant, too,
He brings to me the woodland smelly;
Why should I quote that "village roo,"
      P. Shelley?

I think Felicia Hemans great,
I dote upon Jean Ingelow;
Yet quote from such a reprobate
      As Poe.

To quote from drunkard or from rake
Is not a proper thing to do.
I find the habit hard to break,
      Don't you?

THE PERSISTENT POET

"I remember, I remember"—
  Something special? Not a bit.
But, you see, this is November,
  And Remember rimes with it.

HENCE THESE RIMES

Tho' my verse is exact,
  Tho' it flawlessly flows,
As a matter of fact
  I would rather write prose.

While my harp is in tune,
  And I sing like the birds,
I would really as soon
  Write in straightaway words.

Tho' my songs are as sweet
  As Apollo e'er piped,
And my lines are as neat
  As have ever been typed,

I would rather write prose—
  I prefer it to rime;
It's less hard to compose,
  And it takes me less time.

"Well, if that be the case,"
  You are moved to inquire,
"Why appropriate space
  For extolling your lyre?"

I can only reply
  That this form I elect
'Cause it pleases the eye,
  And I like the effect.

THE OLD ROLLER TOWEL

How dear to this heart is the old roller towel
   Which fond recollection presents to my view.
It hung like a pall on the wall of the washroom,
   And gathered the grime of the linotype crew.
The sink and the soap and the lye that stood by it
   Remain; but the towel is gone past recall.
O tempora! Also, O mores! Sic transit
   The time-honored towel that creaked on the wall.
The grimy old towel, the slimy old towel,
The tacky old towel that hung on the wall.

Now hangs in the washroom a huge roll of paper—
   The old printer's towel we'll never see more.
The new (see directions) is "used like a blotter,"
   And crumpled and scattered in wads on the floor.
And often, when drying my hands in this fashion,
   The tears of remembrance will gather and fall,
And I sigh (though I'm not what you'd call sentimental)
   For the classic old towel that propped up the wall.
The sainted old towel, the tainted old towel,
The gooey old towel that hung on the wall.

UP CULTURE'S HILL

(The confession of a club lady.)

The path up Culture's Hill is steep,
   And weary is the way,
With very little time for sleep
   And none at all for play.

She that this toilsome task essays
   Must never bat an eye,
But keep her firm, unwavering gaze
   Forever fixed on high.

For should she ever careless grow,
   And let her glances stray
Down to the shallow vale below,
   Where Pleasure's Court holds sway—

Lured by the thrice forbidden fruit,

She'd lose her equipoise,
And like a wayward Pleiad shoot
  Down to forbidden joys.

I've been but short time on the road,
  My courage still is strong;
Yet often have I felt the goad
  That hurries me along.

I've fallen over Maeterlinck,
  And bumped myself to tears,
Burne-Jones's pictures made me blink,
  And Wagner hurts my ears.

I've stumbled over Ibsen humps
  And over Rembrandt rocks,
I've got some fierce Debussy bumps,
  Some awful Nietsche knocks.

I'm wearied by the ceaseless quest,
  I'm wayworn and footsore.
I've Culture till I cannot rest—
  Yet still I climb for more.

But oh, when all is done and said,
  Upon some manly breast
I'd like to lay my tired head
  And take a good long rest.

THE PASSIONAL NOTE

"The erotic motive is almost entirely absent from American poetry. Even our younger American poets are more profoundly interested in the why and wherefore of things than in the girdle of Helen or the gleaming limbs of 'the white implacable Aphrodite.'"
                                        —MR. SYLVESTER VIERECK.

In the years of my season erotic,
  When Eros was lord of my days,
And I loved, with a love idiotic,
  The Mabels and Madges and Mays;
When a purple and passionate lyric
  Would sing all the night in my head,—

I yearned, like the young Mr. Viereck,
    For everything red.

I doted on poems of passion,
    And put my own pantings in rime,
To celebrate, after a fashion,
    The damsels who took up my time.
I fed upon Swinburne, believe me,
    I feasted on Byron and Burns,
And couplets from Sappho would give me
    Most exquisite turns.

How apparent it was that our songbirds—
    Our Emerson, Lowell, and Payne,
And Bryant and Drake—were the wrong birds
    To pipe to the passional strain.
There was, in a word, nothing doing
    In all of the rimes that they wrote;
They seemed to be always pursuing
    The ethical note.

What truth, I inquired, was so mighty,
    What ethical thing was so rare,
As the limbs of the white Aphrodite
    Or a strand of her heaven-kissed hair!
The girdle of red-headed Helen
    Outweighed all the wherefores and whys,
And Wisdom elected to dwell in
    A pair of blue eyes.

Now lyrical sizzlers and scorchers
    Fail somehow to set me ablaze;
No longer are exquisite tortures
    Provoked by these passionate lays.
I've tinned—and I can't say I've missed 'em—
    The poems of passion and sin.
Some things one gets out of one's system,
    And other things *in.*

——————————————

L'ENVOI.

"Go, little book," as Poet Southey said;

64

You might be better and you might be worse.
With just one word of warning you are sped:
Remember, you're not Poetry—you're Verse.

www.ingramcontent.com/pod-product-compliance
Lightning Source LLC
Chambersburg PA
CBHW020810020726
47495CB00008B/2674